The TOWN MOUSE

AN AESOP FABLE
ADAPTED AND ILLUSTRATED BY
JANET STEVENS

and the
COUNTRY MOUSE

Holiday House / New York

For TED, *who loves big animals*

Copyright © 1987 by Janet Stevens
All rights reserved
Printed in the United States of America
First Edition

Library of Congress Cataloging-in-Publication Data

Stevens, Janet.
The town mouse and the country mouse.

SUMMARY: A town mouse and a country mouse exchange
visits and discover each is suited to his own home.
    [1. Fables.   2. Mice—Fiction]   I. Title.
II. Country mouse and the city mouse.
PZ8.2.S835Tp   1987   398.2'45293233   [E]   86-14276
ISBN 0-8234-0633-4

Once upon a time, there was a town mouse and a country mouse.
They were cousins.

The country mouse lived in a barn. He got up at sunrise and worked hard all day.

The town mouse lived in a fancy apartment building. She ate breakfast in bed and was very lazy.

One day, the town mouse went to visit her cousin in the country. She swished through the door and flung herself down on the couch.

"What a tiring trip. I'm exhausted and hungry. Where's lunch?" she said.

"Let me take you to the cow," answered her cousin.

When they reached the cow, the town mouse said, "What does the cow have to do with lunch?"

"We're having milk for lunch," said her cousin.

"Ew, milk! I don't drink milk," said the town mouse.

"Well, then, how about some vegetables?" asked her cousin.

The country mouse took the town mouse to the garden.

"You expect me to eat these vegetables raw?" asked the town mouse, turning up her nose.

"Maybe you'd like some bacon and beans from the cat's dish instead," said her cousin.

"From the cat's dish? How disgusting!" sniffed the town mouse. "Let's forget about lunch. Is there anything fun to do around here?"

"We can float down the stream on a leaf and look at the scenery," said her cousin.

"Only if I don't get my feet wet," said the town mouse.

As they floated gently past the shore, the town mouse complained, "This is boring. Take me ashore."

The country mouse tried to think of what would please his cousin.

"I've got it!" he cried. "Let's pull the pig's tail and see if he grunts."

The town mouse took one look at the pig's tail and wrinkled her nose. "I'm not touching *that!* What else can we do?"

"We can sit by the road and wait for a car to go by," suggested the country mouse.

"Only if I don't get my tail dirty," said his cousin.

They sat and they sat and they sat.

Nothing happened.

"This life is too slow for me," declared the town mouse. "I'm going home. Why don't you come with me? I'll show you how *I* live. Then you'll see what the good life is like."

So the town mouse took the country mouse to the city.

When they arrived, the country mouse looked up.

"Where are all the trees?" he asked.

"We don't have many trees. We have tall buildings instead," said the town mouse. "I'll take you up to the top of one."

They climbed and they climbed and they climbed.

Finally they reached the top. The country mouse looked down at the street below and said, "I feel dizzy."

"I know what will make you feel better," said his cousin. "Eating. I'll take you home for dinner."

They rode the elevator down to the first floor and scurried out
to the sidewalk. The country mouse saw feet everywhere.
"Help! I'll be crushed," he cried.
"Don't be silly," said his cousin. "Just keep moving."

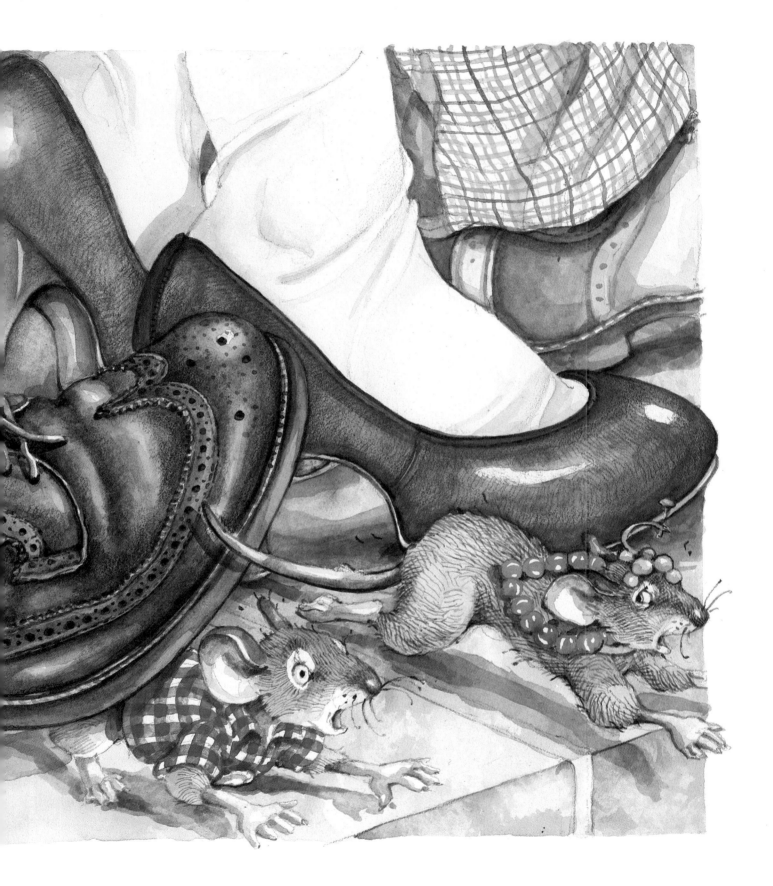

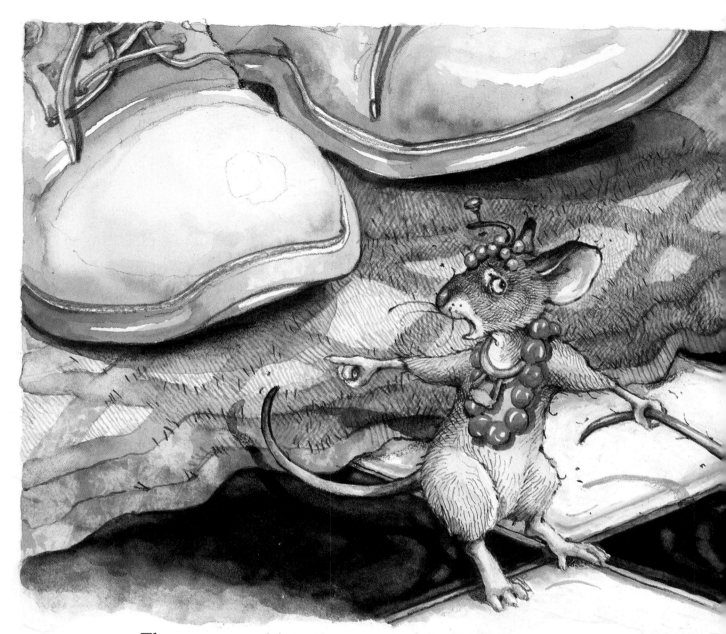

They scampered into the apartment building where the town mouse lived. "Watch out for the mousetrap in the lobby," she warned.

"What's a mousetrap?" asked the country mouse.

"You don't want to know. Just don't touch it," said his cousin.

"But that cheese looks good," said the country mouse.

"Not as good as what's waiting upstairs," said his cousin.

The town mouse took the country mouse to her apartment. In the dining room, they found the remains of a scrumptious dinner party.

"Wow!" exclaimed the country mouse. "Is that all for us?"

"Yes," said his cousin. "Let's start eating."

The two mice gobbled up cakes and cookies, ice cream and pies. The country mouse had never tasted anything so good.

"My tummy hurts," he groaned.

"Eat this chocolate. You'll feel better," said his cousin.

Suddenly, the two mice heard growling and snarling.

The country mouse jumped. "What's that?"

"It's only the watchdogs who live here," said the town mouse.

"Do watchdogs eat mice?" asked her cousin.

"Sometimes," said the town mouse. "You have to be quick to get away."

Just at that moment, the door flew open and two huge dogs came bounding in. The country mouse shrieked and fell into a blueberry pie.

"I'm getting out of here!" he squeaked as he scrambled out of the pie and toward the door.

"What, going so soon?" asked the town mouse.

"Yes!" squealed her cousin, and he headed for home as fast as he could.

When the country mouse got back to his barn, he breathed a
sigh of relief. "I've learned an important lesson," he thought to
himself. "IT'S BETTER TO HAVE BEANS AND BACON IN PEACE THAN
CAKES AND PIES IN FEAR."